This Little Tiger book belongs to:

Here comes the

Kathryn White   Michael Terry

Crocodile

LITTLE TIGER PRESS
London

It was hot in the deep green jungle when Crocodile leapt from the river. He sniffed and snarled, growled and snapped. The jungle shook and quivered. His long tail whipped as he scuttled along. "I want food to make me str**ooo**ng."

Brown Monkey came
swinging down, to Crocodile's
hungry delight. Crocodile snatched
poor Monkey's tail and Monkey
screeched in fright.

"Oh Crocodile don't you eat me or your
sharp teeth will wobble and drop. You'll go skinny
and sag like a crocodile bag and your great jaws will
dribble and flop. I'm made of sickly chocolate,"
Monkey chattered with glee.
          "I knew that," said Crocodile,
          creeping away. "You're too
          small a snack for me."

Crocodile felt hungrier than ever when he spied through his big beady eyes, two flamingos dancing together: "Now here's a tasty surprise." Crocodile sneaked through the water with a hungry glint in his eye. "Two treats I see, as pink as can be, I'll snatch them before they fly."

The flamingos chuckled
and fluffed, "Why, don't
even take one lick.
We're both made of
sugary candyfloss and
are bound to make
you quite sick.
You'd howl and you'd
yowl and you'd grimace.
You'd swell and you'd
tumble and roll."
"I knew that," said Crocodile,
lying, "I've only come out
for a stroll."

Crocodile marched off defeated with a gurgling
hole in his tummy. He spotted an elephant drinking:
"Elephant dinner, yummy." Into the water he slithered
as swift as a snake in the grass.
And when he got to where Elephant was . . .
he leapt up as quick as a flash.

"Oh Crocodile don't you
eat me or your jaws will
jangle and lock.
For it's quite clear to see you
can't eat me for tea because
I am solid grey rock."
"I knew that," said Crocodile
blushing. "You're a boulder
as big as can be. I'm just out
for a walk, no time to talk
as I'm meeting
a dear friend for tea."

"Oh boo hoo!" yowled Crocodile, shedding big tears. "I feel like I haven't eaten in years." He blubbered and bawled and wallowed and squalled. He rolled on his back, which looked very funny, then wailed and hollered, "I want my mummy!"

"Don't worry," said
kindly young Zebra,
"you can share all
my grass with me."
The two pink flamingos
brought treats to share,
with Monkey's
bananas for tea.
"And I've brought some
clear, cool water," said
Elephant trumping a spray.
And Crocodile grinned
with his big sharp teeth
and said, "What a
wonderful day!"

It was hot in the deep green jungle
as the animals played by a tree, when
Tiger leapt out from behind them,
growling, "I am ready for tea!"

Charlie, my inspiration
~ K W

To my son, Jamie,
my little crocodile
~ M T

LITTLE TIGER PRESS
1 The Coda Centre, 189 Munster Road, London SW6 6AW
www.littletiger.co.uk

First published in Great Britain 2004
This edition published 2016

ISBN 978-1-84869-376-0

Printed in China • LTP/1900/1500/0416

2 4 6 8 10 9 7 5 3 1